WITHDRAWN

D0292134

Katherine Applegate

Doggo AND Pupper
SEARCH FOR COZY

illustrated by **Charlie Alder**

Feiwel and Friends

New York

For Lightning, still hissing after all these years.

—KA

For my cozy crew, J & W.

—CA

A Feiwel and Friends Book
An imprint of Macmillan Publishing Group, LLC
120 Broadway, New York, NY 10271
mackids.com

Library of Congress Cataloging-in-Publication Data is available.

First edition, 2023
Feiwel and Friends logo designed by Filomena Tuosto
The artist used a combination of collage and digital
techniques to create the illustrations for this book.
Printed in China by RR Donnelley Asia Printing Solutions Ltd.,
Dongguan City, Guangdong Province

ISBN 978-1-250-62102-3 (hardcover)
1 3 5 7 9 10 8 6 4 2

Contents

Chapter One

Bad News

"Bad news," said Cat. "The humans
had another idea."
    "Uh-oh," said Doggo.
    "Oh no," said Pupper.

"Will there be silly hats?" Doggo asked.
"Will there be bubble baths?" Pupper asked.

"No hats," said Cat. "And no bubbles." She licked a paw. "Worse."

"Will there be fireworks?" Pupper asked. "Or vacuums?"

"Will there be shots?" Doggo asked. "Or nail clippers?"

Cat sighed. "The idea will not bother you, Pupper. Or you, Doggo. Only me."

"I will save you, Cat!" said Pupper. "I am not afraid of anything. Except giant squirrels."

"There is nothing you can do." Cat moaned. "It is too late. The humans went to the pet store. They got me a present."

"But that is a good thing!" said Doggo.
"Was it a toy mouse?"

"Or a bag of treats?" asked Pupper.

"No such luck. The humans got me the worst thing in the whole, wide world," said Cat. She covered her face with her paws. "They got me a new bed."

Chapter Two

The Bad New Bed

Cat showed Doggo and
Pupper the bad new bed.

It was in the
same place as
her old bed.

It was the
same size as
her old bed.

It was the
same color as
her old bed.

BABY CAT ♥

15

"It looks just the same," said Pupper.

Cat shook her head. "My old bed was cozy. It had claw marks. It had bits of fur. It smelled like me."

16

"You do smell nice,
Cat," said Pupper.
"Of course I do,"
said Cat. "I am a cat."

"After a while, the new bed will have your claw marks and fur," said Doggo.

"And your nice smell," said Pupper.

Cat jumped onto the bed. She clawed. She rolled.

She stretched.

"Something is still missing," she said.

"It needs more cozy."

"Where does cozy come from?" Pupper asked.

"You cannot buy cozy," said Cat. "You cannot make it. Cozy just *is*."

She looked out the window. The day was gray. Rain was coming.

"Where will you sleep now, Cat?" asked Doggo.

"I have no choice," said Cat. "I will never sleep again."

23

Chapter Three

A Gray Day

Doggo, Pupper, and
Cat went outside.

26

They said hello
to their yard pals.

27

Worm was gardening.

Bunny was nibbling.

Squirrel was showing off.
(He was not the giant kind.)

It was windy. The clouds were dark and busy.

"I do not see why you are so sad, Cat," said Pupper. "I like getting presents."

"I know the problem."
Doggo winked at
Pupper. "Cat is picky."
"Is that so," said Cat.

31

"Sometimes you are picky, too, Doggo," said Pupper.

"Me?" asked Doggo.

Cat and Pupper looked at each other.

"Well, I am not as bad as Cat," Doggo said.

Cat and Pupper looked at each other again.

33

"I guess everyone is picky sometimes," said Doggo.

"I am only picky about important things," said Cat. Her eyes were sad. "A cat without a place to sleep. What kind of a cat is that?"

Chapter Four

Nap Time

It was nap time.

Doggo was a big fan of naps.

Pupper was not.

41

First Doggo read a story. It was about
three bears and a girl with golden hair.

"That girl is like Cat," said Pupper. "She is looking for just the right bed, too."

Doggo closed his eyes.

"Naps are boring,"
said Pupper.

Doggo snored.

"Naps are for little puppers," said Pupper.

Doggo snored again.

45

"Cat is never going to sleep again," said Pupper. "Why do I have to?"

Doggo opened one eye. "Trust me," he said. "Cat will sleep again. Sleeping is her superpower."

"I wonder where her old bed is,"
said Pupper.

Doggo made an extra-loud snore.

"Doggo," said Pupper. "I know you are not asleep."

Doggo sighed. "Her bed might be in the trash."

"Maybe we can find it," said Pupper. "It would make Cat happy."

"You know what would make *me* happy?" asked Doggo.

"A nap?" Pupper guessed.

Doggo snored.

And this time it was for real.

Chapter Five

Cat Keeps Looking

That night more rain came.
The sky grumbled.
Pupper was glad to have Doggo near.

He was a good thunder friend.

Cat went here
and there.

She looked for a
new place to sleep.

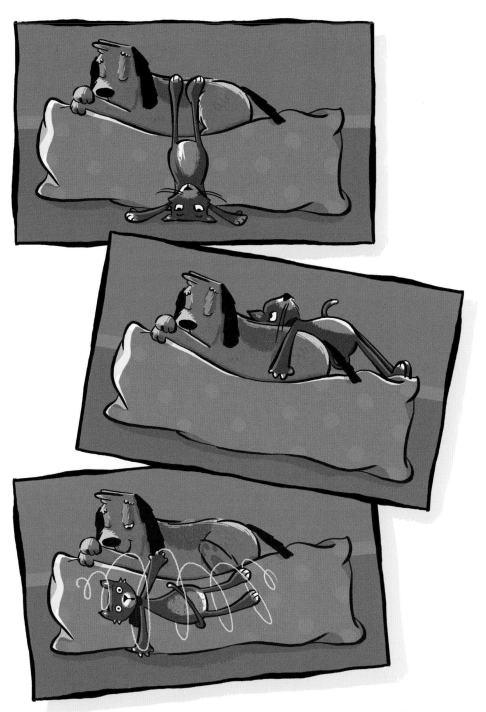

She tried to sleep with Doggo.

She tried to sleep
with Pupper.

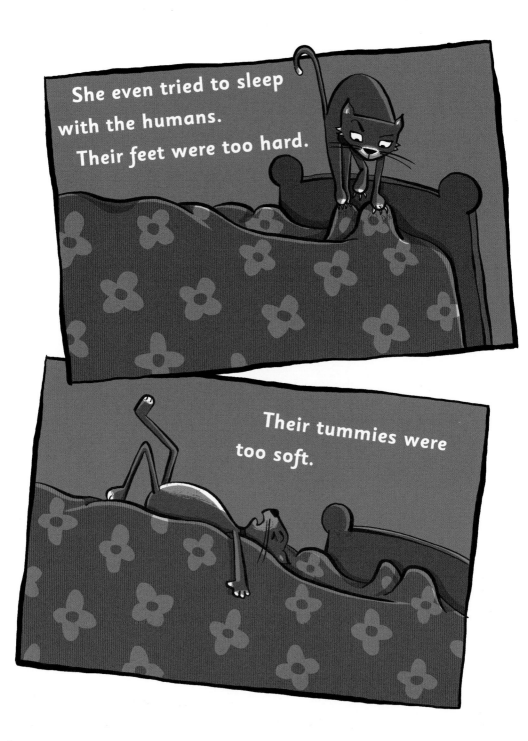

Surprise! Their heads were just right.

Too bad the humans did not agree.

63

Chapter Six

Tricking the Humans

All night Cat prowled.

All night she made
angry sounds.

"I did not sleep," Doggo said in the morning. He yawned. "Because Cat did not sleep."

"We have to find her old bed," Pupper said.

They went
downstairs.

They did not see Cat anywhere.

69

The humans were in the kitchen.

"The garbage cans are outside," said Doggo. "The humans will be mad if we open them."

Pupper smiled. "We will have to trick them."

Doggo went to the kitchen trash can. He grabbed the bag with his teeth. He looked at the humans and wagged his tail.

The humans were glad to have such a helpful pet.

"Sure," they said. "We hate that chore! Let us know if you want more."

Doggo and Pupper pulled the trash through the doggie door.

It was wet outside. The grass was mushy. The bushes were drippy.

It took a long time to dig through the garbage cans. They were smelly. They were messy.

But at last, there was Cat's bed!
Just then, the sun came out.
"Doggo, look!" said Pupper. "A rainbow!"
Doggo smiled. "This was a good idea,
Pupper. Cat is going to be able to sleep
again. And so will we."

Chapter Seven

Finding Cozy

"Wait until the humans go upstairs," said Doggo. "Then we will switch the beds."

"What if they see?" asked Pupper.

"Humans are easy to fool," Doggo said. They waited until the coast was clear.

Doggo and Pupper carried the old good bed to the living room.

The bed was wet. And gooey. And smelly. But it was the bed that Cat wanted.

The new bad bed was on a shelf.

It was next to the window. Sunlight poured in.

It was warm and golden.

Doggo yanked on the bad bed.
Someone yowled.

It was Cat!

"What are you doing?" she cried. "I was sound asleep!"

"I was curled up in a nice little ball. I was dreaming about a cake made of tuna fish."

"We found your old good bed, Cat!"
said Pupper.

Cat looked. "It has old food on it."

"But it has your claw marks,"
said Doggo. "And your fur."

Cat sniffed. "It smells like last
night's dinner."

"But it has your
smell, too," said
Pupper. "And
it has cozy."

"This new bed has cozy, too," said Cat. She smiled at the shining sun. "It just took a while to get here."

Cat curled into a ball again. "The sun. And a new good bed," she said. "I am one lucky cat. Thank you, Pupper. Thank you, Doggo."

"You are welcome," said Pupper.
"And you are good friends," said Cat.
She closed her eyes. "One more thing,
you two," she said.

"I am sorry to tell you that you smell like last night's dinner," said Cat. "You may even need bubble baths."

"Uh-oh," said Doggo.

"Oh no," said Pupper.

"Also," said Cat, "you both have lettuce on your heads."

And then she fell asleep.

Cat's Guide to Napping

Naps are *always* a good idea.

A nice stretch before napping helps.

Squishy pillows are the best.

Do not forget your favorite blanket.

Reading a story can help you sleep.

Grown-ups like naps, too.

Snoring is okay. And so is purring.

Toes need to stay warm.

Naps are even better with friends.

It is always fun to dream about tuna fish cake.